noah ronsyth

The Banana Machine

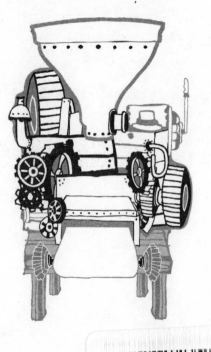

D0416116

The Banana Machine

Alexander McCall Smith

illustrations by Ian Bilbey

BLOOMSBURY

For Natalie, Jonna and Abigail Salvesen

Published in Great Britain in 2006 by Bloomsbury Publishing Plc,
36 Soho Square, London, W1D 3QY

First published by Blackie Children's Books in 1994

Text copyright © 1994 by Alexander McCall Smith
Illustrations copyright © 2006 by Ian Bilbey
The moral rights of the author and illustrator have been asserted

All rights reserved. No part of this publication may be reproduced or
transmitted by any means, electronic, mechanical, photocopying
or otherwise, without the prior permission of the publisher

A CIP catalogue record of this book is available from the British Library

ISBN 0 7475 8052 9
9780747580522

Printed in Great Britain by Clays Ltd, St Ives plc

1 3 5 7 9 10 8 6 4 2

All papers used by Bloomsbury Publishing are natural, recyclable products
made from wood grown in well-managed forests.
The manufacturing processes conform to the environmental
regulations of the country of origin.

www.mccallsmithbooks.co.uk
www.bloomsbury.com

CHAPTER 1
Aunt Bat's Dilemma

What shape are bananas?

What a question! Everybody knows that bananas are curved. They start off curved, they grow curved, and they're still curved when you peel them. That's just the way bananas are.

Patty knew all about bananas. She lived

on a banana plantation, on an island called Jamaica. The banana plantation was owned by her aunt, Aunt Bat. Bat was not her real name, of course, but that's what everybody called her. And it suited her too, though nobody could say exactly why. On the opposite page is a picture of Aunt Bat, with Patty beside her, and Patty's cousin, Mike. Patty was a bit older than Mike, and they were very good friends. And as for Aunt Bat, she was very fond of both Patty and Mike, at least most of the time. Sometimes she got cross with them, and then she would shout with a voice that would shake the banana trees.

'There's that Bat a-hollering again,' the neighbours down the road would say. 'Just like a hurricane's coming! Look out!'

Most of the time, though, Aunt Bat was in a good mood and everybody was happy.

The banana plantation was not very big. In fact, it was one of the smallest banana plantations in that part of Jamaica. It used to belong to Aunt Bat's father, Grandfather Michael, but he had lost quite a bit of it. It might sound odd to lose bits of a banana plantation, but that's exactly what Grandfather Michael had done. And the story of how he lost it was very strange.

Grandfather Michael was a very tall man with a small beard and a smile that stretched all the way across his face. He was very popular in that part of the island, and this was for two reasons. The first of these was that he could tell what the weather would be like for at least two days ahead – and he was never wrong.

'Any chance of rain tomorrow?' people would call out to him as he walked into town.

Grandfather Michael would look up at the sky. Then he would wet a finger and hold it up to find out which direction the wind was coming from. He would scratch his head, think for a moment, and then, 'No rain in the morning,' he might say. 'Then, just back of lunchtime, when you're thinking of having a little sleep, down it'll come. Great big buckets of it until four o'clock. Then it's going to get dry again and the sun will be out till six. Then the sun goes down and the wind comes up from Cuba. Then, next morn-

8

ing, no rain, no clouds, just wind. Will that do you?'

Everybody was always very pleased with these forecasts. Grandfather Michael told them when the wind was going to drop so they could get the new roof on the church without any danger of it being blown away. He warned fishermen about storms, and this probably saved quite a few lives. He also told people when to have weddings so that the guests wouldn't get wet, and when to put on their warmest jersey. It was all very useful information.

Everybody liked Grandfather Michael because of his way with the weather, but also because he liked to play cards. Whenever anybody came to see him, Grandfather Michael would always reach into the top pocket of his waistcoat and draw out a pack of cards.

'How about a game?' he would ask. 'Not a long game – just a quick game. How about it?'

And of course most people couldn't refuse, and they would sit down at a table with Grandfather Michael and play a few hands of rummy or poker. Grandfather Michael liked to bet too, and soon there would be a pile of coins on the table in front of him and the gambling would begin in earnest.

Usually the stakes were quite small. But sometimes Grandfather Michael would get caught up in a game where the stakes were really quite large, and when this happened the piles of money in front of the players grew and grew. Grandfather Michael couldn't resist these occasions and, like most gamblers, he never knew when to stop.

One Sunday, a long time ago, Grandfather Michael was playing a game of poker with some of his neighbours. It was a hot afternoon and they were all sitting around a table under the big sea-grape tree outside the house. Grandfather Michael had not been very lucky, and soon the pile of money he had started out with had dwindled to almost nothing. He was quite sure that his luck would change, so when he was dealt quite a good hand of cards he decided to put all his remaining money on winning that one round. Of course he lost, as gamblers almost always do.

Now that he had no money left, the rules said he had to leave the game and let the other three finish it off by themselves. This annoyed Grandfather Michael, who now had no chance of winning anything back.

'If I could just play two more hands,' he said to himself, 'I could win back everything. I'm certain I could!'

He looked at his neighbours.

'Supposing I bet half my land,' he said calmly, 'will you let me play this round?'

The neighbours were astonished.

'For true?' they asked. 'Do you really mean it?'

Grandfather Michael nodded.

'Look,' he said, 'I'll write down on a piece

of paper, *I promise to give the winner of this piece of paper half of my banana plantation, for true. Signed, in the presence of everybody at the table, Michael.*

The neighbours looked at one another, and then nodded.

'Well, all right,' one of them said. 'But

that's a big risk you're taking there, Michael.'

Grandfather Michael smiled.

'I'll be lucky,' he said. 'Just you watch.'

They dealt out the first cards, and very slowly everybody lifted theirs up to see what they had been dealt. Grandfather Michael's hands should have been shaking, but they weren't. He was as cool as if he were playing for small change.

The dealer looked at the players, and one by one they asked for more cards. When it came to Grandfather Michael's turn, he changed two of his cards, and then stopped. Then, quite calmly, he put his cards down on the table and waited for the bidding to finish.

At last it was time to see everybody's cards and to find out who had the best hand. The air was electric with excitement, and one of the neighbours had to wipe beads of perspiration off his brow. Slowly all the cards were laid on the table.

Everybody looked. Then they looked again. Grandfather Michael had been bluffing all along. He had no good cards in his hand at all. And there on the table, for everyone to see, was the piece of paper with the promise of half his banana plantation on it.

Now there were some neighbours who would have laughed and said, 'No worry. We'd never take away your land.' But the man who had won the land was not like that. He took up the piece of paper, folded it carefully, and put it in his pocket. Then he said, 'That's just fine then. Give me the deeds to the land tomorrow morning.'

Grandfather Michael looked his neighbour in the eye and nodded.

'I promised, and so I will,' he said. 'I'll be over at your place just after eight.'

And so it was that half the banana plantation was lost, and when it passed to Aunt Bat after Grandfather Michael died it was hardly large enough to keep one family.

Because the plantation was so small, Aunt Bat did most of the work, and she was helped by Patty and Mike. Patty and Mike had to go to school, though, and could only help afterwards. So everybody was always busy looking after the trees and trying to make sure the bananas grew as big and healthy as possible.

But even with all this hard work, things were not going well.

'I wish we could get more money for our bananas,' sighed Aunt Bat when she returned from the fruit market in nearby Port Antonio. 'If it goes on like this, I'm afraid we'll have to sell the plantation. I could get a job in town, I suppose. I know people down there who would give me work.'

'But we can't sell this place,' protested Patty. 'We've always lived here! We've always grown bananas!'

Aunt Bat shook her head.

'If the price they pay for bananas gets much lower,' she said, 'it won't be worth growing them any more. We might as well give up.' Over the next few weeks, Patty worked particularly hard. She took great care to see that the trees were watered properly, and she stayed out in the plantation until the moment the sun went down, doing all the chores that had to be done. She cleared dead leaves from the base of the trees and kept an eye out for banana thieves. Aunt Bat was delighted with all Patty's work, but it made her sad to think that it might all be for nothing.

Mike helped as well. Although he was younger than Patty, he was always at hand to do what he could. He enjoyed covering the bunches of bananas with sacking to protect them from the cold at night, and he would also chase away birds which looked as if they might damage the crop.

'I don't want to move,' he said to his cousin. 'I love living here.'

Patty did her best, but when they took the next load of bananas down to the banana merchant in Port Antonio, they were all very disappointed. The price was lower than it had ever been, and this made Aunt Bat shake her head despondently.

'I'm going to have to sell up,' she said. 'It's no use going on.'

The next time she went to town, Aunt Bat asked if anybody was interested in buying the plantation. One man was, and he said that he would come out to look the place over.

'I don't care about the bananas,' he announced. 'I shall probably stop growing them. I shall build myself a new house up there and use it to get away from everything.'

Patty was outraged when she heard this. The thought that the banana trees which her family had worked on for so many years would be allowed to die filled her with anger.

'Please don't sell up just yet,' she pleaded with Aunt Bat. 'You never know what might turn up over the next few weeks.'

Aunt Bat looked very doubtful, but she agreed to wait until a bit more of the crop had been sold before she signed any papers.

'Don't be too hopeful, though,' she warned Patty. 'I don't feel that anything can save the plantation now.'

CHAPTER 2

Patty Has a Brainwave

Over the next few days, Patty racked her brains to think of anything she could do to stop the sale. She wondered whether they could grow something else as well as bananas, but there were several things wrong with that idea. One of them was that there wasn't much land which was not already covered with bananas trees. The other was that it would take months and months before any new crop would be ready for harvesting and sale. And by that time it would be too late.

More bananas were ready for picking now, and Patty went into Port Antonio with her aunt to sell them. Once again, they did not fetch a very good price.

'I have one or two things to do,' said Aunt Bat, after they had left the banana merchant's office. 'Can you do something by yourself for an hour or so?'

Patty was happy to do this, and she was even happier when her aunt fished in her bag and gave her a few dollars.

'Buy yourself an ice cream with this,' she said. 'You deserve it after all your hard work.'

Patty went off to a café near the town centre. It was owned by a cheerful man called Mr Harry, who was well known for making good ice cream. Patty ordered a

chocolate banana special, which was the fanciest ice cream Mr Harry made. It had a topping of chocolate dotted with cherries. And through the middle, there was stuck a large banana, over which more chocolate sauce was poured.

As he was preparing it, Mr Harry chatted with Patty.

'These are tricky things to make,' he said. 'Bananas are the wrong shape for ice-cream cups! It's a pity they don't make a straight banana!'

Patty laughed.

'That would be a good idea,' she said. 'Straight bananas would also fit into lunch-boxes more easily.'

'Yes,' agreed Mr Harry. 'They would be a great improvement all round, surely they would!'

The chocolate banana special was now ready. As Patty dipped her spoon into it, she was still thinking. Why were bananas curved? Most things were straight, or round, but very few things were curved. Although he had been joking, Mr Harry was right. Straight bananas would be altogether much better. Perhaps somebody might invent a way of straightening them.

Patty looked up from her ice cream, her

eyes wide with excitement. *Yes! I could be that person!* she thought. *Why don't I invent a way of straightening bananas?*

As they drove back to the plantation, Patty was still deep in thought.

'You're quiet back there,' said Aunt Bat. 'You sick?'

Patty shook her head.

'I'm just thinking,' she said. 'I've had a good idea.'

'What is it?' asked Aunt Bat inquisitively.

'It's something to do with bananas,' answered Patty. She did not want to say any more, as there was not much she could say about her way of straightening bananas until she had thought of how to do it. And that, she knew, was going to be the difficult part!

When she got home, Patty went straight to her room. Sitting down at her desk, she took a piece of paper out of her drawer and started to sketch. First she drew an ordinary banana. Then, just below it, she drew another banana. That was the easy part.

Patty thought carefully. If something is curved, the way to make it straight is to bend it. But this would not be easy with a banana. She knew very well that if you bend a banana it breaks in two. That's just the way bananas are made.

Patty began to draw again. This time she drew a box, a fairly large one, and inside the box she drew various wheels and levers. They looked like this:

She scratched her head. If the banana went in there, then it would have to go round that wheel there, and then ... What then? Yes, it could slip in between those two pegs while that bit over there, the – well, she would have to get a name for that part – while the whatever it was pushed in that direction. Would that work? She was not at all sure.

After quite a bit more thought, and a lot of head scratching, Patty's drawing was finished. She sat back for a moment, looked at it, and then wrote at the top of it: THE MACHINE FOR STRAIGHTENING BANANAS. Then, underneath that, she wrote: SECRET.

She was very proud of her drawing. But drawing an invention is only part of the business of inventing. The next step is to build the invention and see if it could work. Patty wasn't at all sure if she could manage it. But at least she would try.

Over the next few days, Patty divided her

time between her chores on the plantation and the search for all the parts she would need to make her invention. There was a small workshop on the plantation, and she found some of the parts there, but there were still quite a few bits and pieces that she simply could not find. There were no cogs, for instance, and these were very important. Nor were there any levers of just the right size, and Patty knew that the machine wouldn't stand a chance of working without those.

She was sure that the machine could work, and it seemed a great pity to have to give up on it now. But without the cogs, and some of the other parts she needed, there really seemed little chance of making it go.

If you look hard enough for something, you often find it in the end. And that is what happened to Patty. She searched and searched, poking about in every cupboard and tipping out every cardboard box of old bits and pieces. Then, when she was pouring herself a glass of milk in the kitchen, she noticed Aunt Bat's old mixer lying on the table, and there, in the middle of it, was a cog of just the right size!

'Aunt Bat will never notice if I just borrow this,' Patty said to herself as she unscrewed the cog and put it into her pocket.

And she soon found the other parts. There was a lever which she took out of Aunt Bat's alarm clock, and she also found several very suitable pieces in the piano. Now she had everything, and all she had to do was put it all together.

That afternoon, Patty built her machine. She put a sign outside the workshop saying: NO ENTRY – VERY BUSY! Then, with the plans laid out before her, she assembled all the parts she had gathered. It was a slow business, and very tricky, but at last it was finished. There before her on the workshop table, stood the very first machine of this kind that the world had ever seen, and Patty

had made it all herself! She felt very proud;
but would it work?

She would soon find out.

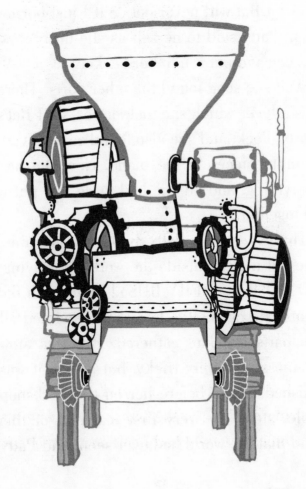

CHAPTER 3

The Plan Goes Square-Shaped

Patty stood back and looked at her machine. It was just as she had imagined it would be – or almost. At one end there was a sort of funnel – where the bananas went in – and at the other end there was a moving belt which the bananas would travel along once they had been straightened in the machine. And in between there was an impressive array of mechanical bits and pieces – wheels, pipes, wires, cogs, flanges, hooks, hoops, snuckers, snickers, snippers and dippers. All in all, it was a very impressive invention indeed!

Patty knew that now was the time to test the machine. It was all very well building a machine like this, but it would be no good at all if it didn't work. And the only way she could find out whether it would work would be to try it out.

Just then, Patty heard her cousin return.

'Mike!' she called from the workshop. 'Come and see!'

Mike, who was crossing the yard when he heard his cousin call him, entered the workshop cautiously. Patty sometimes played tricks on him, and he didn't want to fall into some trap that she had prepared for him.

'What are you doing?' he asked suspiciously. Then, seeing the machine, his mouth opened wide with surprise.

'What's that?' he asked. 'Does it work, whatever it is?'

Patty laid a proud hand on the top of her machine.

'This,' she said, 'is a machine for straightening bananas – that's what it is!'

Mike walked up to the machine and peered at it. Then he looked at his cousin and laughed.

'What's so funny?' asked Patty defensively. 'Don't you believe me?'

'No,' said Mike. 'It's ridiculous. You can't straighten bananas. That's the way they are.'

Patty smiled. 'Do you want to see it work?' she challenged. 'I can easily show you.'

'Good,' said Mike. 'I'll go and fetch a banana. Then we'll really see whether this great machine of yours works.'

Mike soon came back with a bunch of bananas. He chose the biggest, most curved one, and handed it to his cousin.

'There,' he said. 'You just try to straighten that!'

Patty took a deep breath. She felt confident that her machine would work, but she could not be absolutely sure. What if she had installed some of the parts upside down? What if some of the wheels were too small? She would just have to hope for the best.

Patty took the banana and put it into the funnel. Then she took hold of the large handle which operated the machine, and began to turn it round. At first nothing happened, and Mike began to smile knowingly, but after a moment, there came the most peculiar sound. It was a squeezing sound of some sort, but it soon turned into a squeaky sound. Then there was a groaning noise, and after a while a cranking sound as the belt at the end began to move.

'My goodness!' shouted Mike. 'Look! Look!'

There, at the end of the machine, was the large banana. It was no longer curved. Nor was it straight, I'm afraid to say. It had been cut into twenty tiny squares!

'What's the use of that?' Mike crowed triumphantly. 'What a useless machine!'

Patty let go of the handle and the machine ground to a halt. It was a failure! The machine didn't work at all. Perhaps it was too much to hope for that a banana-straightening machine could ever be built. It was very sad.

But Patty did not give up. If she did, she knew there would be no chance of saving their banana plantation. She would try again. She would take the machine to bits, examine all the parts, and try to build it again, properly this time.

In the meantime, Aunt Bat had become very puzzled. Her alarm clock had not gone off that morning, and she had slept in. Then, when she had gone downstairs to make her morning cup of tea, she had noticed that the teapot had no lid. And when she had tried to bake a cake, and had reached for her mixer, she had discovered that it no longer worked. It was all very strange.

'Patty,' said Aunt Bat, in a puzzled voice. 'Something very strange is going on in this house. Do you know anything about it?'

Patty stared at her aunt. 'Something very

strange, Aunt Bat?' she said. 'Are you sure
you aren't imagining things?'

'My eyes aren't playing tricks on me,'
retorted Aunt Bat. 'The teapot lid just got up
and walked out of the house, all neat and
easy, and as for my mixer . . .'

Patty gulped.

'I'm sure these things can't be far away,'
she said. 'I'm sure they'll come back.'

Aunt Bat snorted.

'It all seems mighty strange to me,' she said, looking suspiciously at her niece.

Over the next few days, Patty carefully took the machine to pieces and laid out each part on the workshop bench. Then she examined the plan to see where she had gone wrong. Everything seemed to be in order, as far as she could see. The hinges were all in the right places – yes, here they were, and they fitted well. And these screws, the long ones with the twirly tops, they were right too. Yes, they went in like this and came out the other side just like that. Where could she have gone wrong? It was all very baffling.

Then she noticed it. The cog she had taken from the mixer seemed as if it was the right shape, but when you looked at it from underneath you could see that there was a problem. When it turned, it scraped against another part, and that went wrong too. So that was it!

Now Patty knew exactly what she had to

do. She had to find a cog which was about the same size as the one she already had, but with a slightly different shape. But where could she find one?

Suddenly the idea came to her. Aunt Bat had a car, an old car which she very seldom used. Patty had seen the engine once, and she remembered that it was full of all sorts of pipes and wires and ... cogs. She was sure that she could find one the right size there and just, well, just *borrow* it for a little while. Later on, when she had made enough straight bananas, she could put it back and the car would work just as well.

Patty lost no time in carrying out her plan. Making sure that Aunt Bat was nowhere to be seen, she slipped out into the yard and made her way to the place where the old car was kept. Then, trying not to make too much noise, she opened the bonnet of the car, propped it open with a stick, and looked inside.

It was just as she had remembered it.

There were hundreds of wires running all over the place, and any amount of piping. And there were cogs too! There were at least ten of them!

Patty soon found a cog of just the right size. Carefully she took it out of the engine and closed the bonnet. Then, cradling the precious part in her hands, she went straight back to the workshop and began to put the banana machine together again. There would be no mistakes this time. It was bound to work. It had to.

CHAPTER 4
Car Trouble

'Mike!' shouted Patty. 'Come here quick!'

Mike was soon at the door of the workshop, peering in at his cousin.

'I've fixed it,' said Patty proudly. 'It's ready.'

Mike laughed. 'That silly old machine?' he mocked. 'Do you really think that it's going to work?'

'It's not a silly old machine,' Patty said hotly. 'And it *will* work! Just you see!'

'Try it then,' challenged Mike. 'I'll go and fetch a banana.'

As Mike ran off to pick a banana, Patty gave the machine a quick polish. She was sure that everything fitted exactly, and it should work now – at least, according to the plan it should work. But she knew that even the best plans sometimes went wrong, and she was prepared for another disappointment.

Mike returned with a long, very curved banana. Patty took it from him and put it into the funnel. Then, her heart beating hard with excitement, she began to turn the handle. Inside the banana machine, she heard the cogs and levers begin to move. She saw the belt begin to turn and the banana disappear as the machine sucked it down into its works.

Patty closed her eyes. She did not want to see the banana emerging from the other end, neatly chopped into little pieces. She did not want to see it peeled, or squashed, or mashed into a sticky brown mess.

'Look!' shouted Mike suddenly. 'Patty! Look!'

Patty opened her eyes. There, at the other end, was the banana. And it was no longer curved, as it had been when she had put it in. It was perfectly, completely, and without the slightest bit of doubt – straight!

'Straight as a ruler!' cried Patty triumphantly. 'Look! The very first straight banana!'

Both Patty and Mike knew that they had seen something very important. They had seen the making of the first straight banana in the history of the world, and for a moment they did not know what to say. Then Patty broke the silence.

'Now,' she said, 'we must make a few more straight bananas and take them to Port Antonio. We can show them to Mr Harry and ask him what to do.'

'We'll be able to sell them,' said Mike excitedly. 'Everybody will want to buy them.'

'It'll save the plantation,' Patty said. 'We'll have the most unusual bananas in the world. We won't be able to grow enough of them!'

'What about Aunt Bat?' asked Mike. 'What will she think about it?'

Patty was silent for a moment.

'We can tell her about it,' she said. 'I'm sure she'll be pleased.'

She paused. 'There's one thing I don't want her to know, though. Can you keep it secret – just for the time being?'

Mike nodded, and so Patty told him about the cog which she had borrowed from Aunt Bat's car. She explained that she would put it back sooner or later, and that Aunt Bat would never notice as she hardly ever used the car.

'Don't forget to put it back,' Mike warned his cousin.

'I won't,' she reassured him. 'Now let's go

and show Aunt Bat the world's first straight banana!'

'I don't believe it!' said Aunt Bat, shaking her head. 'I just don't believe it!'

'But it's true,' said Mike. 'Patty's invented a machine for straightening bananas, and this is the very first one it straightened.'

Aunt Bat picked up the banana and examined it.

'It looks fine from the outside,' she said. 'But what about the inside? Bananas turn black on the inside if you squash them. How do you know it's going to be all right underneath?'

Patty's face fell. 'I hadn't thought … I mean, I don't know,' she said lamely. It would be terrible if she had gone to all that trouble only to invent a machine that ruined perfectly good bananas.

'Well, let's see,' said Aunt Bat, and she began to peel the straight banana.

Patty held her breath. She hardly dared look at the banana as it emerged from its skin. But there it was at last – perfect and unharmed.

'There's nothing wrong with this banana,' said Aunt Bat. 'This really is amazing!'

The three of them each took a bite from the straight banana. It tasted like any other banana, but somehow it seemed easier to eat. You didn't have to hold the banana at an angle to eat it – you could just point it straight at your mouth. It was very simple.

Aunt Bat listened as Patty told her of how Mr Harry had first planted the idea in her mind, and of how she hoped that they would be able to sell their straight bananas for a better price. Aunt Bat nodded her approval.

'It can't do any harm,' she said. 'And it might do a lot of good. But what we must do first is make a whole heap of straight bananas. Then we can take them down to Port Antonio and set up a stall in the market. We can paint a large sign saying, STRAIGHT BANANAS, and see what happens.'

'Yes,' agreed Patty. 'And we can tell the newspaper to come and take a photograph. Everybody will hear of our straight bananas if we do that.'

Over the next few days, they all worked very hard for the launch of the straight bananas. Aunt Bat drew the lettering for the sign, which Patty then painted in, and they

45

all took turns at putting curved bananas in one end of the machine and getting straight ones out at the other. It was quite exhausting turning the handle, but at last everything was ready.

On the morning of the launch they had breakfast early. Aunt Bat had telephoned the newspaper in Port Antonio and they agreed to send a reporter and photographer down to the market at nine o'clock. They had to eat their breakfast quickly so that they could load up the truck for the journey.

Then Aunt Bat made her announcement.

'Since it's such a special day,' she said. 'We can travel down to Port Antonio in my car. There's plenty of room for the bananas in the back, and it will be much more comfortable than making the journey in that bumpy old truck.'

Mike glanced at Patty, whose jaw dropped at the news.

'I'd much prefer to go in the truck,' she protested. 'Wouldn't you, Mike?'

Mike nodded vigorously. 'We always go in the truck,' he said. 'I don't want to change.'

'Well, I'm driving,' said Aunt Bat, 'and I've decided. So don't you go arguing with me. We're going in the car!'

As Aunt Bat left the room, Patty whispered to her cousin. 'Don't worry,' she said. 'I'll take the cog out and put it back in the car. You keep her busy. Show her something. I'll fix the car while you're distracting her.'

Mike thought quickly. He could hear Aunt Bat in the kitchen and he knew that in a few minutes she would be ready to set off for town. He wondered if he could pretend to be ill? That might delay things a bit.

He walked into the kitchen, trying hard to look sick.

'Aunt Bat,' he said. 'I'm not feeling too good.'

Aunt Bat carried on with what she was doing.

'You looked fine to me at breakfast,' she said. 'And you surely ate enough.'

Mike looked down at the floor.

'I was fine then,' he said. 'Now I feel a little bit … I feel a little strange.'

Aunt Bat threw him a glance.

'Oh, yes,' she said. 'You got something wrong with your stomach then? Too much food?'

'No,' he said. 'Well, maybe it is a bit funny. Maybe it's something I ate.'

Aunt Bat returned to her kitchen tasks.

'You'll soon feel better,' she said. 'Wait until your breakfast's gone down, then you'll feel just fine again.'

Mike groaned.

'But I'm not at all well,' he said. 'I think I'm really sick.'

And with that he made a gurgling sound and sat down on one of the chairs in the kitchen. This made Aunt Bat pay attention.

'That's not a good sound,' she said. 'Maybe I should take a look at you.'

Meanwhile, out in the workshop, Patty had removed the cog from the banana-straightening machine and had run across to the place where Aunt Bat's old car was parked. Wasting no time, she opened the bonnet of the car and started to fit the cog back where she had taken it from. It was a tight fit and she wondered whether she was putting it in the right place.

'I'm sure it came from there,' she murmured to herself. 'It was just in there. Just behind that bit that sticks out.'

She tightened one or two bolts and screwed in several screws. Then, checking up that no parts were left over, she quietly shut the bonnet, wiped her hands on a piece of rag, and ran back to the house.

When Patty went into the kitchen, she saw a miserable Mike sitting at the table while Aunt Bat was pouring out a hefty dose of liquid from a large green bottle. Patty stopped in her tracks. It was Aunt Bat's home-made tonic, what she called her 'cure-everything'. It was made out of old mangoes, lemon juice, the leaves of various plants, and clove after clove of garlic. It smelled indescribable, and it tasted even worse. Aunt Bat swore that it could cure just about anything, although she only administered it to the children when she thought they really needed it.

'Not the tonic!' Patty blurted out, as the foul smell of the evil-looking liquid reached her nose.

Mike looked up sharply. He was clearly relieved that she had arrived. Now he could stop pretending to be ill and they could go out to the car without any fear of Patty being caught out.

'I'm feeling better,' he said, jumping to his feet. 'I'm much, much better.'

'Sit down,' snapped Aunt Bat. 'You said you felt really sick. This mixture will fix you. You sit down and open your mouth.'

'But I'm better,' shouted Mike. 'I promise you I am. I'm completely better. I'm one hundred per cent again.'

'I don't think so,' said Aunt Bat. 'I didn't

like the look of your tongue when I had a quick peek at it just then. You open wide and swallow.'

Mike was trapped. Closing his eyes as tightly as he could, he opened his mouth for the large spoonful of the frightful mixture and winced as he swallowed it.

'Aargh!' he said, as the foul-tasting liquid ran down his throat. Then, for a moment or two, he could say nothing. There were no words to express the taste of Aunt Bat's cure-everything; only a shocked silence would do.

Now Aunt Bat turned to face Patty.

'Your turn,' she said. 'Open wide.'

Patty's mouth opened – in shock.

'Me?' she stuttered. 'But I'm not ill. I never said that I was feeling sick. I'm fine. I promise I am.'

Aunt Bat shook her head.

'You may think you're fine,' she said. 'But I know what these bugs are like. They make Mike feel ill and in two licks they're making

you sick too. You take this just to protect
you from what your cousin's got. Come on
now, open wide.'

And she advanced towards Patty with
another spoonful of the stink mixture. Patty
was trapped too. She opened wide, swallowed, and then let out a scream.

'Don't make such a fuss,' chided Aunt Bat. 'Look, you watch me take my dose. You don't see me making a fuss.'

The two children watched their aunt pour out an especially large dose for herself. Then she opened her mouth and poured the liquid down her throat.

'Wonderful,' she said, as she wiped her mouth. 'That stuff tastes just fine. I don't know what all this fuss is about, I really don't!'

The two children helped Aunt Bat to load the boxes of straight bananas into the back of the car.

'Did you put it back?' whispered Mike to Patty. 'Will it go?'

Patty nodded. She was not sure whether everything would be all right. She hoped it would, but she had ended up feeling very unhappy about one of those screws.

With the bananas loaded, Aunt Bat got into the driving seat, while Patty and Mike slipped in beside her. It was a very old car, with a strange smell about it, but Patty always enjoyed travelling in it. But would they be doing any travelling today, she wondered?

'Right,' said Aunt Bat cheerfully. 'Off we go!'

She put the key into the ignition, checked that the car was not in gear, and pressed the starter button.

Immediately, and without any hesitation, the engine roared into life. Patty's jaw dropped with amazement, and she turned to Mike, who grinned.

'What's so funny?' asked Aunt Bat, glancing at her nephew.

'Er … nothing,' said Mike. 'I'm just a little bit surprised that the car started so easily. You hardly ever use it.'

'It never lets me down,' said Aunt Bat proudly, slipping the engine into gear. 'It's a wonderful car this. It would still go even if half its engine fell out!'

At this, Patty dug Mike in the ribs, and it

was all that the two children could do to stop bursting out into fits of laughter.

They drove out of the plantation and down on to the main road. A truck passed them going in the other direction and the driver, a friend of Aunt Bat's, waved and sounded his horn. Shortly after that, things began to go wrong.

At first Patty thought Aunt Bat must have pressed the accelerator pedal too vigorously. Suddenly, and without any warning, the car leapt ahead as if somebody had attached a rocket to it.

Aunt Bat gave a start, and immediately took her foot off the pedal. The car slowed down again, but the moment she touched the pedal again it surged forward, the engine roaring mightily.

'Slow down, Aunt Bat!' urged Patty. 'We'll go off the road!'

'It's not me,' snapped Aunt Bat. 'Something's got into this car's head this morning. It thinks it's a racing car.'

As she spoke, the old car began to pick up speed again. Aunt Bat wrestled with the steering wheel, trying to keep them from flying off the road, her mouth a thin line of determination.

'Watch out!' shouted Patty, as they shot past a man leading two goats along the road.

They sped past the surprised man in a cloud of dust. The goats gave a leap and dragged him off the road on to the grass verge. Patty turned round to see the man shaking his fist at the retreating back of the car.

'Road hog!' the man shouted. 'Lunatic!'

By the time they reached the town, they were all thoroughly shaken up. Patty closed her eyes as they covered the last few yards of the journey, and only opened them again when she felt the car come to a final stop.

'Well,' said Aunt Bat, adjusting her hat. 'Something has happened to the engine. It's never run so well in all its life. Remember how we used to have difficulty getting up the hills in this old crate? Now we'll just sail up them!'

Patty thought that it was now time for her to confess.

'It's me,' she said. 'I mean, it's my fault. I fiddled with the engine, you see …'

'Well done!' said Aunt Bat. 'No mechanic on the island could have done that to my poor old car! You've given her a whole new lease of life!'

They unloaded the boxes of bananas and carried them to the market. Aunt Bat had a friend there who had said that she could use part of her stall, and it was here that the newspaper reporter and the photographer were waiting.

'Is this a joke?' asked the reporter sourly. 'I've been told to come down here and see some sort of new banana. They said something about straight bananas.'

'It's not very funny,' chipped in the photographer. 'I've got far better things to do with my time than take photographs of practical jokes!'

'You wait and see,' said Aunt Bat sternly. 'You won't believe what we've got!'

The straight bananas had all been wrapped in a large sheet so that nobody could see them before they were ready to be unveiled. Now, with the bundle in position on the stall table, Aunt Bat clapped her hands to attract the attention of passers-by. The market place was already quite busy, and a small crowd of people rapidly drifted over to find out what the excitement was all about.

'Ladies and gentlemen,' Aunt Bat began. 'What you are about to see is truly, truly historic. Never before has Jamaica seen anything quite like this. In fact, never before has anything like this been seen in the whole world!'

'Sales talk!' jeered one of the members of the crowd. 'You higglers try to sell us any old thing and you call it something special. You can't fool us!'

'Oh yes?' challenged Aunt Bat. 'Well, just you wait and see!'

And with that, she gestured to Patty and Mike to pull the sheet off the bananas.

'The world's first straight bananas!' shouted Aunt Bat. 'Just you look at that!'

For a moment, there was silence. The reporter took a step forward and peered at one of the bananas. Then a member of the crowd came up and did the same.

'My goodness!' exclaimed the reporter. 'They really are! They're straight bananas!'

That was the signal for a tremendous surge. Everybody wanted to buy one, and before a few minutes had passed, every single straight banana (except for two which Patty was saving) had been bought, examined, and in some cases, eaten.

Aunt Bat looked at Patty and Mike and winked.

'It looks like I'm not going to have to sell up after all,' she said, adding, 'thanks to you, Patty!'

While Aunt Bat and Mike went shopping after the successful banana sale, Patty took the last two straight bananas and ran as fast as she could to Mr Harry's café. Mr Harry could tell that Patty was excited.

'Good news?' he asked.

'Yes,' said Patty. 'I've got some very good news.'

'Well, tell me, then,' urged Mr Harry. 'I could do with some good news.'

Patty reached into her pocket and took out the two straight bananas. With a flourish of pride, she laid them down on the counter in front of the café owner.

'You remember how we talked about a straight banana, and how useful it would be?' she paused, watching the expression on Mr Harry's face. 'Well, here it is!'

Mr Harry picked up one of the bananas and let out a whistle.

'I had no idea,' he said. 'I had no idea it could be done.'

After Mr Harry had thoroughly examined the bananas, he told Patty to wait while he fixed up something special. A few minutes later, he came out of his back room with two large glasses full of ice cream, chocolate sauce, cherries, and, of course, the straight bananas.

'Here we are!' he said triumphantly, passing one of the glasses to Patty. 'The very first *straight*-banana double-chocolate special!'

That would have been a perfect end to the

day, but unfortunately things were not to work out quite like that. After she left Mr Harry, Patty met Mike and Aunt Bat and they all got back into the car. The engine started perfectly and Aunt Bat slipped the vehicle into gear. But, as they started to move, everything went wrong.

Instead of going forwards, the car went backwards.

'You're in reverse,' yelled Mike, who saw that they were heading straight for a tree.

Aunt Bat slammed on the brakes and fiddled with the gear lever again.

'That's funny,' she said. 'I'm sure I was in first gear.'

She tried again, but exactly the same thing happened. She stopped, changed gear, and tried once more. But it was no use. The car would only go backwards.

'We're going to have to drive home like this,' Aunt Bat sighed. 'You two turn round and look out of the back window. Tell me where I'm going and I'll steer.'

The two children crouched on the back seat and looked out of the small rear window.

'Left hand down,' called out Mike, as the car set off erratically. 'No, not that much! Right hand up. No, down!'

And so they continued on their way. It was, thought Mike, the most frightening journey he had ever done. They almost went over a cliff – twice – and on several occasions they drove straight into ditches and out the other side. But eventually they got home in one piece and Aunt Bat turned off the engine. They all sighed with relief, and Mike and Patty found it strange to be walking into the house forwards. Somehow they were still thinking backwards, and it was not until a good hour later that everything seemed normal again.

Patty summoned up all her courage and explained to Aunt Bat all about the car. She told her aunt about the cog, and how she had put it back, but not very well. Then she looked down at the floor, waiting for her aunt to explode.

Aunt Bat laughed.

'So that was the problem,' she said. 'Well, well!'

'You're not vexed?' ventured Patty. 'You're not going to shout at me?'

'Oh no,' said Aunt Bat. 'I think you should just take the cog out of that car again and put it in the machine. It's more use there. But mind you put it the right way round, though. You wouldn't want that machine of yours to run backwards now, would you?'

CHAPTER 5

Success!

The next day, the story of the straight bananas was splattered across the front page of the newspaper.

GIRL INVENTS STRAIGHT BANANA! proclaimed the headline. LOCAL GIRL PROVES THAT BANANAS NEED NOT BE BENT!

There was a photograph of Aunt Bat selling a straight banana, with Patty and Mike smiling at her side. Then there was a close-up photograph of one of the straight bananas, with an ordinary curved one beside it, just to show the difference.

Aunt Bat was very pleased with her photograph, and she glowed with pride when the neighbours stopped by and congratulated her.

'You're getting famous these days, Bat,' they said. 'Hope you don't get too grand for us.'

'No danger of that,' Aunt Bat assured them, and gave everybody one of the new straight bananas which Patty had prepared.

There were telephone calls too. There was one from Mr Harry, who asked Patty whether she could give him a regular supply of straight bananas so that he could announce to his customers the arrival of the straight-banana special. Patty asked Aunt Bat, who readily agreed to that. Then there was a call from the mayor himself, who asked for some straight bananas to be sent to the town office so they could be shown to important visitors. And finally, there came a call from the big hotel on the bay, where all the rich visitors stayed.

'We'll pay you double the price of ordinary bananas,' said the man from the hotel. 'Or, make that three times the price. Is that enough? But we would like a supply this afternoon, please.'

Patty and Mike redoubled their efforts with the banana machine, and by lunchtime they had made a large enough pile to satisfy all the orders they had received. Aunt Bat lent a hand too, although she was busy picking fresh bananas from the tree to make sure that there were enough to go into the machine.

That afternoon, the customers all came round for their bananas. Mr Harry fetched his, and left a large carton of ice cream as a special thank-you present. The mayor's assistant called to collect theirs, and was pleased when he saw that Patty had selected the very straightest ones for him. Then, last of all, people arrived to collect the big order for the hotel.

Soon, all the straight bananas had gone. Patty and Mike sat at the kitchen table, quite exhausted. Aunt Bat was tired too. In fact, she was too tired even to make supper. And so all they had to eat was a bun with a slice of cheese.

'We'll have to get to bed early,' said Aunt Bat, yawning. 'There are lots of bananas to straighten tomorrow and we'll need all the rest we can get.'

'Mmm,' said Patty drowsily.

Mike said nothing. He was already asleep, a half-eaten bun on the table before him.

That night, Mike had a nightmare. It was not like the normal nightmare, where you imagine that you're in a dark wood or where you imagine that you're trying to run away from some frightening creature; this was a nightmare about bananas.

In the dream, Mike was standing in the yard with a large pile of bananas in front of him. He put these into the machine and turned the handle, but no matter how hard he turned, no bananas came out of the other end. His arm was aching with the effort, and he was panting to get his breath back, but there seemed to be no way of persuading the machine to work. Suddenly, all the bananas he had fed into the machine began to shoot out like cannonballs out of a cannon. Up they went into the air, twisting and turning, before falling down like descending rockets. In the meantime, there was a crowd of angry customers forming a line behind him.

'Where are our bananas?' they chanted. 'Give us our bananas!'

Mike felt utterly helpless. His poor, tired arms were too exhausted to work any more, and the machine was still firing bananas out in every direction. He never wanted to see another banana, he thought, neither straight nor curved. He had had enough.

Aunt Bat woke the children extra early the following morning. They ate their breakfast hungrily, and then went straight out to the workshop to begin work on the bananas.

They took it in turns to work the machine. While Patty struggled to turn the handle, Mike could push bananas into the funnel. Then, when a pile of bananas had been straightened, they would swap places and Patty would push bananas in as Mike turned the handle. And all the while Aunt Bat would be running to and fro, picking bananas for the children to straighten.

By lunchtime they had prepared another pile, but no sooner had they done this than Mr Harry arrived.

'I must get more straight bananas,' he said. 'Everybody's wanting them now. There's a line of people outside my café, and every single one of them wants a new straight-banana special!'

He took every straight banana there was, and made them promise to have more ready for him first thing the next morning. Then, just when Mr Harry had driven off, a truck arrived all the way from Kingston, the capital on the other side of the island.

'We've heard all about your famous bananas,' said the driver. 'My boss says you're to sell me all you've got.'

Patty shrugged her shoulders. 'But we've just sold the last of them,' she said. 'It takes a long time to get them ready.'

'Then I'll wait,' said the driver. 'I've got plenty of time. And my boss says I'm not to come back without a full load of straight bananas!'

So, while the driver sat under a tree and watched them working, Patty, Mike and Aunt Bat redoubled their efforts. At last, just before sunset, they had enough to sell to the driver, and he was satisfied.

'Thanks a lot,' he called out as he drove off. 'I'll come back for more tomorrow!'

Patty looked at Mike and they both sighed. Both had sore arms from turning the handle of the machine, and Aunt Bat was bent almost double from the effort of lifting all those bananas.

'We'll never manage to do enough,' said

Patty miserably, as they sat down with exhaustion.

'But we'll have to,' said Mike. 'Mr Harry wants more tomorrow and that driver said he's coming back too.'

'And there are lots of other orders,' sighed Aunt Bat.

'We'll have to start even earlier,' said Patty. 'And then we'll just have to work a bit faster.'

The next day they worked from the moment the sun came up, and didn't even stop for breakfast. More people arrived to buy straight bananas, and no sooner had they prepared a pile of them than they would be snatched off by some eager customer. And at the end of the day, each of them had such sore arms that they could hardly turn the handle of the machine.

'I can't go on,' wailed Mike. 'My arms will drop off if I turn this handle one more time!'

Patty took over from him and allowed her cousin to rest, but her arms were just as

sore, and she found that she was turning the handle so slowly that the machine hardly worked.

'We're going to have to stop,' she said to Aunt Bat. 'I'm ready to drop.'

Aunt Bat nodded her head rather slowly, as she hardly had enough energy even for that.

'You're right,' she said. 'It was a wonderful idea, and a wonderful invention. But it's just too much hard work. We can't do it.'

They sat down where they were, right outside the workshop, and looked at their feet. They were too tired to talk any more, and they were sitting in complete silence when Mr Harry arrived.

Mr Harry could tell at once that something was wrong, and he listened as Patty told him just how tired they were and how they couldn't ever make enough straight bananas to satisfy their customers.

Mr Harry rubbed his chin. He thought for a moment, and then he smiled.

'But it's simple,' he said. 'You don't need to worry.'

They all looked at him curiously, waiting for him to explain.

'The machine needs to be automatic,' Mr Harry went on. 'If you attach an engine to it, then all you do is bring the bananas to it. The machine does the rest.'

Nobody said anything. It seemed a very good idea and both Aunt Bat and Mike looked at Patty. She was the inventor, after all.

'Well, Patty?' said Aunt Bat. 'Don't you think Mr Harry's right?'

Patty shrugged her shoulders. 'Yes,' she said. 'But I'm not sure how I could possibly ...'

She stopped. She had had another idea.

'Aunt Bat,' she said. 'Could you drive your car over to the workshop?'

Aunt Bat looked surprised.

'Why?' she asked.

'Because I've had an idea,' said Patty, rising to her feet. 'And this idea is going to save us a lot of effort!'

Aunt Bat moved the car. Since Patty had removed the cog altogether, the car had stopped going backwards and went sideways instead! This made it very difficult for her to get it to the precise place where Patty wanted it, but at last, after a lot of careful driving, she ended up next to the banana machine. Then she and Mr Harry sat and watched while Patty and Mike got to work. Mike passed screwdrivers to Patty, and took them back when she had finished. Then he passed her spanners and hammers, and several other tools that she needed.

Patty worked away, humming as she did so. Aunt Bat looked alarmed as she saw bits and pieces being taken out of the engine of her car, but Mr Harry told her not to complain.

'Patty knows what she's doing,' he said calmly. 'We'll just watch.'

Patty hoped Mr Harry was right. This was a much more difficult task than the first building of the machine, and she was not quite sure whether it would work. What she had to do was to connect the banana-straightening machine to the car, so that the engine would drive the machine. It was a simple idea really, but she was not so sure how easy it would be actually to do it.

But at last it was finished, and she stood back.

'I think I've done it,' she said, mopping at her oily brow with a cloth which Mike had passed her.

'Done what?' snapped Aunt Bat suspiciously. 'Ruined my car?'

'No,' said Patty. 'I haven't ruined it. I've just changed it.'

'Changed it into what?' asked Aunt Bat, her voice sounding rather alarmed.

'Into a banana-straightening machine,' said Patty. 'Into an *automatic* banana-straightening machine!'

Mr Harry was most excited.

'Let me try it out,' he said. 'You all stand back in case it goes wrong.'

Patty told him how to operate the machine, and then Mr Harry climbed into the car and prepared to start the engine.

'Put a banana into the funnel first,' called out Patty. 'Then switch on the switch.'

Mr Harry selected a large curved banana

and stuffed it into the funnel of the machine. Then he reached for the switch that would bring the car engine to life.

'Here goes,' he shouted. 'Let's see what happens now!'

As he turned the key, the old car gave a shudder. Then the engine came to life, and a very strange, gurgling noise was heard. In a flash, the banana which had been sticking out of the funnel was sucked into the works and before anybody could do so much as blink, out it came at the other end.

'It's straight!' shouted Patty. 'Look! It's straight!'

'Quick,' yelled Mr Harry. 'Fetch more bananas.'

Mike and Aunt Bat ran off to get a supply of bananas and were soon back with several large bunches.

'Put them in,' shouted Mr Harry. 'Put them all in at the same time.'

As the bananas were put into the funnel they were immediately sucked away. And once again, in no more than a second or two, out they came, all perfectly straight.

Aunt Bat rose to her feet and did a little dance of joy. Then she picked Patty up in her arms and hugged her.

'Oh, Patty,' she said. 'You're a genius! A genius!'

Now that Patty had built an automatic banana straightener, they had no trouble in straightening as many bananas as were needed. In fact, it took no more than ten minutes to do a whole day's supply, and the rest of the day would then be free. Slowly their muscles stopped aching, and the hard work of the last few days became little more than a memory.

Aunt Bat was thrilled. The straight bananas continued to sell – at a very good price – and soon the banana-straightening machine became quite famous throughout the country, and even in other countries as well.

There were some people, of course, who

thought that it would all be a nine-day-wonder and that everyone would soon forget all about the straight bananas.

'They'll soon want to go back to curved bananas,' these people said. 'You wait and see.'

Patty and Mike waited to see if this would happen, but it didn't. In fact, it soon became clear that there were all sorts of uses for straight bananas – uses which they would never have dreamed of when they first invented them.

There was a man, for example, who introduced the first 'Banana Dog'. This was for people who liked hot dogs, but who had got a bit tired of them and wanted something different. It's very difficult, as you know, to fit a curved banana into a long, thin roll. It's quite easy, though, to fit a straight one in, and this is just what he did. Banana Dogs were a great success, and soon everybody wanted one.

Then there was the man who invented a

banana slicer. He had tried for years to invent this, but he had always failed.

'It just won't work with curved bananas,' he said. 'But now that I can get straight bananas it works perfectly well!'

And he was right. The new banana slicer chopped straight bananas into rings which were all exactly the same thickness. It was a great help for people who had to slice up bananas to put them in fruit salads.

Aunt Bat took the money from the sale of the straight bananas to the bank and opened a special account to put it in. Each day, after she had sold the latest consignment of the unusual fruit, she would go to the bank and count out the takings with the manager. Bank managers are usually very pleased when people bring large amounts of money into their bank, and this bank manager was no exception.

'What are you going to do with all this cash, Bat?' he asked cheerfully. 'Are you going to buy yourself a new car now that your old one's been made into a banana-straightening machine?'

Aunt Bat shook her head.

'No,' she said. 'I've got a much better plan for it. You'll see soon enough.'

After a few months, when all that season's crop was sold, Aunt Bat went into the bank, checked up how much money she had saved, and then went straight off to the neighbour who had won half the plantation in the game of cards. He was a very old man now, and Aunt Bat had not talked to him since the day Grandfather Michael had announced the result of that disastrous game of cards. She felt that it had been very cruel of him to keep Grandfather Michael to his promise, particularly when the neighbour already had so much land that he hardly knew what to do with it.

Aunt Bat invited Patty and Mike to go with her.

'There's something I want you to see,' she said. 'This is a day I've been waiting for for years and years and I'd like you to come with me.'

She did not explain what she was going to do, and it came as a great surprise to Patty and Mike when they drove in Aunt Bat's truck up the long dust road that led to the neighbour's house.

'But I thought you never talked to him,' Patty said. 'What are you going to say?'

Aunt Bat laughed. 'There comes a time when you've got to speak to everybody,' she said. 'Even those you didn't think you'd ever talk to.'

They parked the truck and walked up to the verandah of the house. The owner was sitting on a swinging chair, staring at them, smiling.

'Well, well,' he called out as they climbed up the small wooden stairs to the verandah. 'So it's my friend Bat come to talk to me after fifteen years. You must have a lot to say, Bat, what with fifteen years and all. Lots of things happen in fifteen years! You come and tell me about some of them.'

Patty could tell that Aunt Bat was furious, but realised she was determined not to show it.

'It's a pleasure to be visiting you, Mr

Johnson,' said Aunt Bat through tight lips. 'I'm sorry my feet never blessed your yard in – how much? In fifteen years? My goodness, how time flies.'

'Well, you just come and sit down here, and the kids too, and we can have a good talk,' said the old man, cackling with laughter. 'I've got all the time in the world these days.'

'Yes,' muttered Aunt Bat, just loudly enough for the children to hear. 'And all the land in the world too.'

'You said something, Bat?' snapped the owner. 'You said something about land?'

Aunt Bat looked straight into the old man's eyes.

'Yes,' she said. 'That land. We all know how you got it. Now I want to ask you: will you sell it back to me? You don't really need it, do you?'

The old man smiled, sitting back in his chair and folding his arms.

'How do you know I don't need it?' he

challenged her. 'I may not grow anything on it, but I just like looking at it. And there's nothing wrong in that, is there? Or is it some sort of new sin to enjoy looking at your land?'

Aunt Bat remained quite calm.

'All I'm asking is, will you sell it back to me? It's a simple question.'

The smile faded from the old man's face.

'All right,' he said. 'You ask a simple question and you get a simple answer. I will sell it back to you.'

'How much?' asked Bat.

The old man smiled again and reached in his pocket for a notebook. Tearing a page out of it, he scribbled down a figure and passed the paper to Bat.

'There,' he said. 'That's my price. And no arguing. You pay that and the land's yours. I promise you.'

Aunt Bat looked at the figure on the piece of paper. It was far too large – almost twice what the land was worth – and she realised

immediately that the old man had chosen a sum which he thought she would never be able to pay. He was playing with her really, and the thought made her fume.

'All right,' she said simply, tucking the paper into her pocket. 'I'll go to the bank tomorrow and arrange for the money to be paid to you. Then you can hand the deeds over, or should I say hand them *back*.'

The old man was astonished.

'You mean you've got the money to pay me what I asked?' he stuttered. 'Where did you get it?'

'Have you heard of the straight bananas?' chipped in Patty. 'Everybody's buying them, you know.'

The old man wrinkled his nose with disgust.

'I don't know,' he said. 'I wasn't really serious. Maybe I don't want to sell that land after all.'

Aunt Bat stood up.

'You gave your word,' she said. 'You gave

me your word in front of these two children here. If you change your mind, then nobody on the island will ever believe you again. They'll call you a liar today, tomorrow, and even when you've gone. Then they'll write on your gravestone, "Here lies a liar." Is that what you want?'

The old man was silent for a moment. Then he spoke.

'I'll meet you at the bank tomorrow. And I want cash, mind you – no cheques – just cash.'

'You'll get it,' said Bat. 'You'll get it in cash, every last cent of it.'

They got the land back, as promised. It was not in very good condition, as it had not been properly farmed for years. But there were still banana trees there, and some wonderful other fruit that had just been allowed to grow wild.

Over the next few weeks they all worked particularly hard, clearing away weeds and sorting things out. Mike dug new ditches for water to flow along and Patty made a path that led through the tangle of trees. It was slow work, and very hard, but at last it began to look less like a jungle and more like a proper banana plantation again.

In the meantime, of course, the straight banana business went from strength to strength. The straight bananas became even more famous, and Aunt Bat's photograph was in all the papers, along with pictures of Patty and Mike. Visitors to the island often called at the house just to see them, and sometimes asked if they could have their photographs taken standing next to Patty, the inventor of the straight banana.

Patty was very modest about all this. She did not want any reward for inventing the machine; she was happy enough that her aunt's problems had been solved and that they could all continue to live on the plantation as they always had done. Her real reward was to be allowed to deliver Mr Harry's supply of straight bananas and to have a free straight-banana double-chocolate special ice cream afterwards.

And it was while she was eating one of these that Mr Harry said something that made her think.

'You know, Patty,' he said. 'I've often wondered why they don't make a special *round* banana to fit on round plates. Then you could put ice cream in the hole in the middle and the banana would keep it from melting too quickly.'

'Do you mean a banana shaped like a doughnut?' asked Patty.

'Ee-hee,' said Mr Harry. 'That would be a pretty useful sort of banana.'

Patty said nothing for a moment. She was busy thinking!